Dear mouse friends,
Welcome to the world of

Geronimo Stilton

THE RODENT'S GAZETTE
EDITORIAL STAFF

Geronimo Stilton
A learned and brainy
mouse; editor of
The Rodent's Gazette

Thea Stilton
Geronimo's sister and
special correspondent at
The Rodent's Gazette

Trap Stilton
An awful joker;
Geronimo's cousin and
owner of the store
Cheap Junk for Less

Benjamin Stilton
A sweet and loving
nine-year-old mouse;
Geronimo's favorite
nephew

Geronimo Stilton

GERONIMO ON ICE!

Scholastic Inc.

Published by Scholastic Inc., *Publishers since 1920,* 557 Broadway, New York, NY 10012. SCHOLASTIC and associated logos are trademarks and/or registered trademarks of Scholastic Inc.

ISBN 978-1-338-30621-7

Text by Geronimo Stilton
Original title *Il segreto dei pattini d'argento*
Cover by Roberto Ronchi, Alessandro Muscillo, and Andrea Cavallini
Illustrations by Danilo Loizedda and Daria Cerchi
Graphics by Michela Battaglin

Special thanks to Tracey West
Translated by Andrea Schaffer
Interior design by Kevin Callahan / BNGO Books

10 9 8 7 6 5 4 3 2 1   19 20 21 22 23

Printed in the U.S.A.   40

First printing 2019

A CITY AS BEAUTIFUL AS A FAIRY TALE!

It was a brisk **winter** afternoon in New Mouse City. Freshly fallen snow decorated the trees and buildings, **SPARKLING** in the sunlight. The streets twinkled with **HOLIDAY** lights, making my city look as beautiful as a **fairy tale**!

Oh, I forgot to introduce myself! My name is Stilton, *Geronimo Stilton*, and I run *The Rodent's Gazette*, the most famous **NEWSPAPER** on Mouse Island!

The snow is beautiful!

The *ice skating rink* in New Mouse City was frozen solid, so my nephew Benjamin and my niece Trappy asked me to take them. I agreed, of course, but I made sure to **bundle up** against the cold. This is what I wore:

- a heavy jacket . . .
- a wool shirt and a fleece shirt . . .
- wool long johns . . .
- thermal tights . . .
- a pair of super-insulated pants . . .
- four pairs of socks . . .
- four pairs of gloves . . .
- a knitted cover for my tail . . .
- a wool beanie . . .
- a cheddar-yellow scarf . . .
- a pair of very warm snow boots . . .
- earmuffs made of fake fur . . .

I had so much CLOTHING on that I couldn't

move a whisker! So I unpeeled some layers and headed out with the mouselets. We took the **subway** to get to the skating **pond**. During the trip, Trappy pulled on my sleeve.

"Uncle G, after we skate, can we get a **hot chocolate**?" she asked.

Benjamin pulled on my other sleeve. "Uncle G, will you take our **picture** while we skate?"

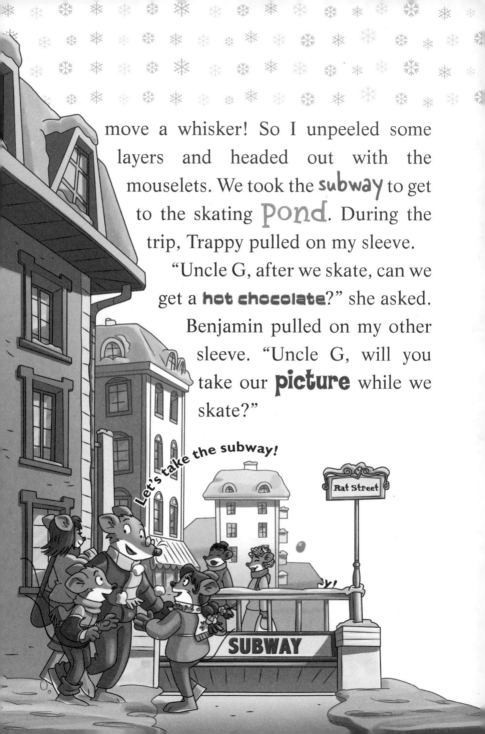

Let's take the subway!

Rat Street

SUBWAY

We left the subway station and entered the enormouse city park. As we approached the **skating pond**, we saw a building with a sign that read, Ice Skate Rentals.

I rented skates for Benjamin and Trappy.

"Have fun skating," said the rodent at the counter. "Now that the Mouse Island Ice Skating Championships are

coming up, everyone is excited about the sport!" he said.

We walked over to the pond. Mice were having fun all over the park. Some were sledding down a snowy hill. Others were building a **snowmouse**. And a group of mice were singing Christmas carols.

Trappy sat down on a bench and put on her skates.

"Benjamin, bet I can skate faster than you!" she squeaked.

"Maybe, but I can **spin** better!" he replied.

Look at us, Uncle G!

Let's spin!

Then the two of them skated onto the ice, yelling, "Look at us, Uncle G!"

"I'm watching you!" I called out, waving. "You are really good!"

"Maybe someday I'll be as great as Lobelia Tutu," Trappy said. "She's going to *win* the championships!"

Benjamin skated past her. "No, I think the mysterious Masked Skaters will win!" he said.

I realized that I didn't know much about the **Mouse Island Ice Skating Championships**, so I picked up a copy of *The Rodent's Gazette* and turned to the sports section.

Then my cell phone rang: **Ring riiiing riiiiiinnnng!**

It was Creepella von Cacklefur, my friend who has a bit of a crush on me. "Hello,

The Secret of the Silver Skates

The Prestigious Prize!

It is time for the Mouse Island Ice Skating Championships! This year, there is a lot of excitement surrounding the couples category because the winners will receive a unique prize: the Silver Skates!

These antique skates are legendary in the world of ice skating. They belonged to the famous skater Olga Goudanov, and were given to her by the Czar Mousoloff, the ruler of Mousekow. Legend says that the

Olga Goudanov's famous Silver Skates were discovered in an attic and turned over to the Mouse Island Skating Commission.

skates contain the clues to where a royal treasure is hidden!

There are five pairs of skaters competing in the couples round: Lobelia Tutu and Shane Shivers; Anastasia Goudanov and Paolo Pivot; Felicia Frost and Axel Spinner; Bella Twirlytail and Johnny Twizzle; and finally, two mysterious competitors known only as the Masked Skaters (no one knows for sure who they are).

Olga invented a spectacular move: "Flight of the Gouda." Impressed by her talent, Czar Mousoloff gave her a pair of silver skates.

Gerrykins? Do you like ice skating?"

"I don't know how to skate," I admitted. "But I like to watch it!"

Creepella shrieked, "Perfect! I have two tickets to the **championships**! Would you like to come with me?!"

"R-r-really?" I stuttered. "I thought I would watch it from my warm, cozy house. I can get very chilly at the ice arena."

Hello, Gerrykins?

"Oh, that's too bad, Gerrykins," Creepella said, with **MISCHIEF** in her voice. "I guess I'll just have to take someone else.

"Which one of my many admirers shall I bring with me?" she asked. "Maybe Baron von Slick, the daredevil pilot? Or Count Sylvania, the most popular

GERONIMO IS NOT MY ONLY ADMIRER. I HAVE **MANY MORE!** I KEEP TRACK OF THEM AND THE GIFTS THEY GIVE ME SO THAT I CAN SEND THEM THANK-YOU NOTES.

MY ADMIRERS

Sal Cemeterius — HAT

Glen Ghoulson — GLOVES

Sir Francis Longfur — BRACELET

Gavin Gloomytail — GLASSES

Baron von Slick — SWEETS

Count Sylvania — PERFUME

Byron Novello — BOOK

Mort Diggermouse — FLOWERS

Gulliver Graybeard — RING

Prince Harold the Horrible — RING

Gaspar Ghostine — FLOWERS

Alvin Testerly

Milo Mysterio — PERFUME

Felix Bloomfur

rodent in Mysterious Valley? Or maybe Sal Cemeterius, the largest producer of **COFFINS** on Mouse Island? Who should I call, Gerrykins?"

"Ahem," I said with a *cough*. "Maybe I can come with you after all. If I dress **warmly**, I should be fine."

"Perfect!" Creepella exclaimed. "It will be so *exciting*! You can pick me up the day of the championships. Bye-byeee!" Then she ended the call.

I sighed. I could not say no to that **mysterious** mouse. She is a very good friend, after all!

Um...

ARE YOU THE MASKED SKATERS?

After I talked to Creepella, I noticed two mice **spinning** on the ice with more skill and speed than any of the others. They wore strange skating costumes decorated with a yellow banana print. One of the two waved at me. I squinted. Did I know him? I did know him, and I knew him well.

HERCULE POIRAT IS ONE OF MY GREAT FRIENDS. WE HAVE KNOWN EACH OTHER SINCE WE WERE YOUNG MICE. HE IS ALSO THE MOST RESPECTED PRIVATE INVESTIGATOR IN NEW MOUSE CITY. SOMETIMES HIS COUSIN BRUTELLA POIRAT ASSISTS HIM.

Very well, actually. It was my dear friend **Hercule Poirat**, the private investigator.

The other skater was his cousin Brutella Poirat. She blew me a kiss.

Hercule skated as fast as LIGHTNING toward me and did a triple turn, landing very close to my tail. "Careful!" I yelled.

Brutella sped toward me and came to a sudden stop a millimeter from my whiskers, covering me in a cloud of ice shavings.

"What are you doing here, and why are you dressed like that?" I asked.

"What's the matter, don't you like our banana costumes?" Brutella asked.

They both began to *SKATE* around me in circles. What were they up to? All I knew was that they were making me dizzy!

Then Hercule whispered in my ear, "We're UNDERCOVER."

"**UNDERCOVER?**" I asked. "Why?"

"Someone is trying to steal the *Silver Skates*!" Brutella said.

I gasped, and Hercule continued telling the story.

"The skates were in the office of the director of the ice arena, and somebody tried to **break in**," he explained. "The director thinks the thief is an ice skater. So he asked us to work **UNDERCOVER** to keep a close eye on them."

My head began to spin. "Let me get this straight," I said. "Somebody tried to steal the Silver Skates. And you are **UNDERCOVER** to protect them. Does that mean you are the **MASKED SKATERS**?"

Benjamin and Trappy heard me and skated over.

"Are you the mysterious **MASKED SKATERS**?" Trappy asked.

"I know you! You're Hercule and Brutella Poirat!" Benjamin yelled.

Someone tried to steal the Silver Skates!

Hmmm . . .

"Shhh," Hercule warned. "You'll give away our SECRET."

But it was too late. "Those mice with the banana outfits are the mysterious MASKED SKATERS!" someone yelled.

A crowd of rodents quickly gathered around us.

"Excuse me, MASKED SKATER, can we take a photo with you?" a young mouse asked Brutella.

Can I have your autograph?

Ahem . . .

Oh no!

I shooed away the crowd. "Get moving! Nothing to see here!" I told them.

"We've been **DISCOVERED**!" Hercule wailed. "This stinks worse than moldy cheese!"

"It's a disaster!" Brutella agreed. "If we can't go UNDERCOVER, we can't keep an eye on the *Silver Skates*."

I nodded. "Of course, of course . . ."

Hercule stroked his whiskers. "Unless we can find **two** rodents who will take our place as the mysterious **Masked Skaters**!" he said.

I nodded again. "Makes sense, makes sense . . ."

He looked at me. "We need someone who knows something about mysteries!"

I agreed. "True, true . . ."

Brutella hugged me. "That someone is **you**, Geronimo!" she cried.

"Obviously, obviously," I said. And then I realized what I had said. "What? Why me?"

Benjamin and Trappy squeaked with **excitement**.

"Go, Uncle G!" Benjamin cheered. "You will be the new **Masked Skater**!"

I protested, "But I don't know how to skate!"

"You can't give up before you even try!" Trappy said.

Hercule pushed me. "Let's rent you some skates so you can start **training**!"

Come on, Geronimo . . .

Argh!

DON'T BE A LITTLE MOZZARELLA!

I put on the skates and then staggered toward the lake with the help of Benjamin and Trappy.

"I'm not sure if this is a good idea!" I squeaked. "I don't have any **BALANCE**!"

"Geronimo, don't be a little mozzarella!" Hercule said. "I know you can do this!"

Go, Uncle G!

You'll see; it's easy!

Most cheeses age for a long time. But **mozzarella** cheese does not take long to make. So when a rodent calls you a mozzarella, it means you are a rookie, an amateur, and also not very skilled!

I didn't want to be a **mozzarella**.

The first time I skated onto the ice, I *slipped* backward, landing on my tail! **BAM!**

My niece and nephew helped me get up.

"Don't give up, Uncle G!" Benjamin said.

I tried a second time and I *slipped* forward, landing on my snout and squishing all my whiskers! **Splat!**

"Don't give up,

Geronimo!" Hercule urged. "Right now you're a mozzarella, but I know that with some training you can be a fine, aged, prize-winning cheddar!"

So I tried for a third time. I fell again and slipped away on my belly like a penguin! Swish!

"Heeeelp, stop me!" I yelled.

The other rodents on the ice heard me.

Slow down, Geronimo!

"Isn't that Geronimo Stilton, the famous journalist?" someone asked. "*What a mozzarella!*"

I kept *sliding* across the lake at super speed, and I only stopped when I *slammed* into a pile of snow at the edge of the lake. *Whomp!*

"I told you I didn't have any *balance*!" I wailed.

That's Stilton!

Watch out!

Stop meeee!

Benjamin and Trappy ran to my rescue. They pulled me out of the pile of snow by the paws. My fur was FROZEN, my whiskers were crumpled, and icicles were coming out of my snout!

When I shook the snow off my eyes, I could see Hercule talking on his banana-shaped phone.

"Hello, **Thea**?" he asked. (Thea, as you probably know, is my sister.)

"**Psst** . . . it's us, Hercule and Brutella."

Pull harder!

I'm trying!

He was trying to whisper, but I could hear every word. "**Psst** . . . *Hello, Thea?* we know that you are friends with Lobelia Tutu . . . **Psst** . . . We need her help. The situation is desperate. Your brother is such a **mozzarella**! *Argh!* What . . . ? You say you know that already? You say not to worry about it? You say that you'll handle it? Okay, see you tomorrow!"

Hercule hung up and turned to me. "Geronimo, we found you a trainer—the **BEST TRAINER** in the city. Her name is Lobelia Tutu!"

THE DE-MOZZARELLA COURSE

The next day, Hercule and Brutella picked me up in their **Bananamobile** and took me to the New Mouse City Ice Arena. Thea and Lobelia Tutu were waiting for us there.

Lobelia was a famouse ice skater. She was a very talented mouse and always wore her Mouslympic gold medal around her neck.

"Thea told me that the situation is desperate," she said. "So, which one of you is the little mozzarella?"

Thea and Hercule pointed to me. "Him!" they said.

"Don't worry," Lobelia told me.

LOBELIA TUTU

A world champion ice skater, Lobelia also teaches skating to mice and offers "intensive courses in de-mozzarellization for desperate cases of mozzarella-itis."

She lives with her grandmother Aurelia and her two sisters: classical dancer Topelia, and professional gymnast Amelia.

"Train with me and I will de-mozzarella you . . . **I swear on my tail!**"

"We need to de-mozzarella him before the championships start," Hercule said. "The *Silver Skates* are in danger!"

"Squeak!" Lobelia exclaimed. "That only gives us a few days. We will have to begin an intensive de-mozzarella course!"

I didn't like the sound of that. "What exactly happens in the intensive de-mozzarella course?"

"You'll find out very soon, Mr. Stilton—I mean **Little Mozzarella**," she said. And even though she was tiny, she sounded very tough. "You can count on that!"

Thea, Hercule, and Brutella started to leave.

"Have a good de-mozzarellization!" my sister said.

"Please, don't **ABANDON** me!" I begged.

We all entered the arena. The ice sparkled under the bright lights hanging from the ceiling.

"*Oooooooooooooooh!*" I exclaimed as I gazed around.

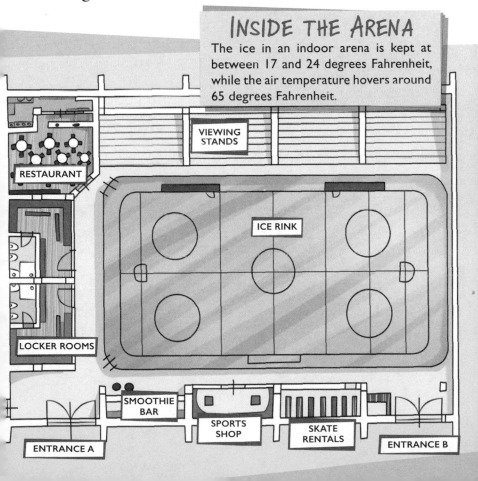

INSIDE THE ARENA
The ice in an indoor arena is kept at between 17 and 24 degrees Fahrenheit, while the air temperature hovers around 65 degrees Fahrenheit.

RESTAURANT

VIEWING STANDS

ICE RINK

LOCKER ROOMS

SMOOTHIE BAR

SPORTS SHOP

SKATE RENTALS

ENTRANCE A

ENTRANCE B

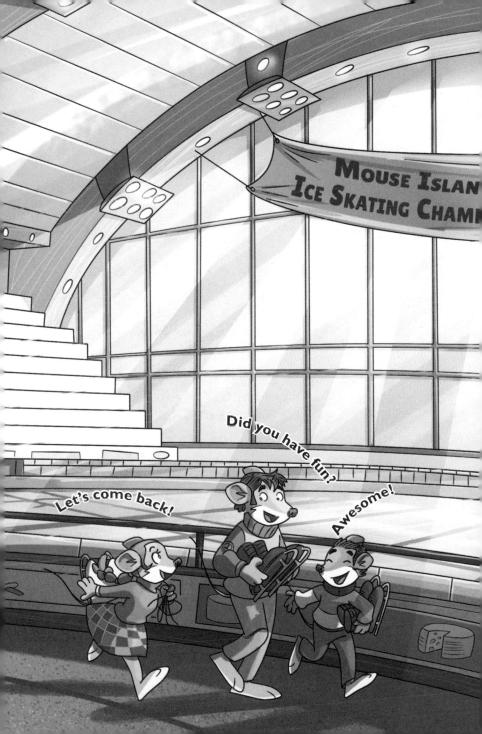

Lobelia **turned** toward me, her paws on her hips.

"So, let's hear it, Geronimo. What level of mozzarella are you?" she asked.

"How would I know?" I replied.

She pointed to a **poster** on the wall.

WHAT
LEVEL OF MOZZARELLA
ARE YOU?

1 You can skate, but you **CAN'T DO TRICKS**.

2 You can skate, but you're a **BIT SHAKY**.

3 You can skate, but you fall **ONCE IN A WHILE**.

4 You fall on your tail **ALL THE TIME**.

5 As soon as you put a skate on the ice, you **SLIP** across the rink on your stomach **LIKE A PENGUIN**!

I cleared my throat. "Then I am a **LEVEL FIVE** mozzarella."

"The situation is more desperate than I *thought*!" she said. "We have a lot of **work** to do, Geronimo!"

"We do?" I asked.

"Don't worry," she said. "I will make sure we get your MOZZARELLA LEVEL down before the competition."

"But this is a COUPLES competition," Hercule reminded her. "He needs a skating partner!"

"What? You didn't say anything about a partner," I said nervously. "Who will want to skate with me?"

Thea smiled. "I know someone who would love to skate with you," she said. "Actually, she would MUMMIFY you if you skated with anyone else."

She took out her cell phone and made a call. "Hello, it's me, Thea. Come right away to the ice arena! Geronimo needs you . . ."

The reply blasted from Thea's phone. "I'm coming!"

I Do Not Look Good in Ruffles!

Ten minutes later, a **PURPLE** convertible **hearse** parked in front of the arena with a loud **screech**. Just as I thought, Thea had called CREEPELLA VON CACKLEFUR!

Thanks, Creepella!

Good to see you!

Lobelia ran up and gave Creepella a hug.

"I haven't seen you in so long!" Creepella said. "Not since we took ice skating LESSONS together when we were just mouselets."

"Those days were so much fun," Lobelia said. "Back then, who would have guessed that I would become a famouse *ICE SKATING* champion and you would become a SUCCESSFUL JOURNALIST?"

Creepella smiled. "Yes, look at us now!"

Lobelia glanced at me. "I heard that you and *Geronimo* are dating. That's so lovely."

I **blushed**. "Well, we are v-v-very good friends," I stuttered.

Luckily for me, Hercule and Brutella walked up just then.

"Lobelia and Geronimo need to get to **work**," Hercule said. "He is a LEVEL

FIVE MOZZARELLA when it comes to ice skating!"

Creepella waved her paw. "Training can wait," she said. "As serious as it is to be a level five mozzarella, we have something more important to do. If we must dress as MASKED SKATERS, we will need the right costumes! Let's all jump into my hearse so we can go shopping."

We all knew better than to argue with Creepella. So we hopped into her hearse and she drove us to RATTOSPORT, the largest sporting goods store in New Mouse City.

In the ice skating department, a friendly salesmouse approached us. "Hello! How can I help you?" she asked.

Lobelia pointed at me and Creepella. "These two need matching ice skating costumes."

The salesmouse clapped her paws together. "Matching costumes! That's so **romantic**! I have some wonderful outfits for you to try on."

Before I could **squeak** that our outfits did not have to be romantic, the salesmouse dragged me across the room. Thea pushed me into a dressing room and Creepella passed me the first outfit.

"I think this one will look **fabumouse** on you, Gerrykins," she said.

"Don't keep us waiting, Geronimo!" Thea called out. "Let's see how you **LOOK**!"

I looked down at what I was wearing and sighed.

"Okay," I said, "but I am only doing it to save the *Silver Skates*!"

I came out of the dressing room wearing a black skating suit with a **flame** design on the chest and a fringe of red and gold beads hanging from the sleeves.

SPICY CHEESE DIP

"This is the **Spicy Cheese Dip** outfit designed by the famouse designer, Tom Fuzzy!" announced the salesmouse.

"Gerrykins, you look delicious!" Creepella said.

"It's so stiff!" I complained. "I won't be able to move in this!"

"Get him another one!" Lobelia said.

I went back into the dressing room and came back out a few minutes later wearing white tights, a pink shirt, and a gold vest that sparkled with sequins.

GOLDEN PRINCE

"Geronimo is wearing the *GOLDEN PRINCE* outfit from the Fairy Tales on Ice collection by Princessa Provolone," the salesmouse said.

"Geronimo, you look so handsome!" Creepella exclaimed.

"Squeak!" I protested. "These sequins are **TOO SHINY**!"

Lobelia sighed. "You are very picky for a mozzarella, Geronimo. Try on another one, then!"

I went back into the dressing room.

A few minutes later, I emerged wearing a skating outfit made of layers and layers of white and blue ruffles.

"Geronimo is wearing Rhapsody in Ruffles

from the renowned designer Christian Furriano," the salesmouse explained.

"More like **ridiculous** ruffles!" I muttered.

"But, Geronimo, you look so charming!" Creepella said.

I shook my head. "I will not be seen in public like this."

RHAPSODY IN RUFFLES

Lobelia put her paws on her hips. "Geronimo, you don't seem to like anything. What outfit would make you **happy**?"

"Isn't there something more classic and less **flashy**?" I asked.

"And purple," Creepella added. "It's my favorite color!"

"I have just the thing," the salesmouse said. "Classic, not flashy, and purple. Let me get you **Bats of the Night** from designer Vampira Vox."

VIOLET SILK BLOUSE

AMETHYST CROWN

SHIRT WITH BAT WING SLEEVES

VIOLET SILK SKIRT

PURPLE VELVET VEST

BELT WITH PURPLE SEQUINS

VIOLET SATIN PANTS

WHITE SKATES

BLACK SKATES

BATS OF THE NIGHT

The salesmouse left and quickly returned with wonderful **PURPLE** outfits for Creepella and me. My shirt even had sleeves that looked like *bat wings*!

We tried on our costumes and modeled them for everyone.

"How **romantic** you look!" Thea said. "Let me take your picture."

"You know, that would be a great photo for your wedding invitations," Lobelia remarked.

"Wedding? We are j-j-just good friends!" I stuttered.

"You really are a beautiful couple," the salesmouse said with a dreamy sigh.

Luckily, Hercule came to my *rescue* again and changed the subject.

"Just one minute," he said. "These costumes are not complete!"

"That's right," Brutella agreed. "You can't be **Masked Skaters** without masks."

"I have exactly what you need!" the salesmouse exclaimed.

She darted off again and came back with two purple satin **MASKS**.

Lobelia happily clapped her paws together.

"Perfect!" she said. "And now that you've got your costume, Geronimo, it's time to de-mozzarella you!"

THE MASKED SKATERS

MY NAME IS
SHANE SHIVERS

When we returned to the ice arena, a tall, thin rodent was waiting for us. He wore a blue skating costume that matched Lobelia's, and he had shiny fur and a thin mustache. On his chest was a Mouslympic **GOLD MEDAL**.

"This is *Shane Shivers*, my skating partner," Lobelia introduced us. "He's going to **help** me train you, Geronimo."

Shane shook our paws.

SHANE SHIVERS

"They told me that the *Silver Skates* are in danger of being stolen. I am happy to help keep them safe!"

We headed over to the ice rink where many skating couples were practicing. One couple stood out. The male mouse was as **BIG** as an armoire and had dark brown hair, and his partner was slim with **fiery** red hair.

PAOLO PIVOT

Lobelia saw me looking at them. "That's *Anastasia Goudanov* and **Paolo Pivot**," she whispered. "They made it into the finals because the members of their rival team were **MYSTERIOUSLY** injured before the

ANASTASIA GOUDANOV

competition. Something about that stinks worse than rotten cheese!"

"Isn't Anastasia Goudanov the great-

THE FINALISTS OF THE
MOUSE ISLAND ICE SKATING
CHAMPIONSHIPS

Anastasia Goudanov

Paolo Pivot

Bella Twirlytail

Johnny Twizzle

Lobelia Tutu

Shane Shivers

Felicia Frost

Masked Skaters

Axel Spinner

great-great-niece of Olga Goudanov?" Creepella asked.

"That is what she claims," Lobelia replied. "Anastasia BELIEVES the Silver Skates belong to her. But Olga's will was very clear: she wanted the skates to go only to the best skaters on Mouse Island."

Shane nodded. "That's why Anastasia entered the championships."

DAILY SCANDAL

ANASTASIA GOUDANOV

DEMANDS THE SILVER SKATES!

THE CHAMPIONSHIP COMMITTEE REFUSES!

BY SAMANTHA TATTLETAIL

The famouse descendent of Olga Goudanov has entered the Mouse City Ice Skating Championships. "I will win the Silver Skates at any cost! I am the best!" she says.

"Enough **SQUEAKING** about Anastasia!" Lobelia said. "We came here to train and we have **SOOOOOOO** much work to do. But you can do it, Geronimo, I know you can!"

"You just need to learn a few simple moves," Shane said, and then he began to rattle off a bunch of moves that sounded **SOOOOOOO** complicated.

"No problem! We can do that," Creepella responded.

But I was in a cold sweat!

How would I be able to learn all those moves in such a short time? I couldn't even stand on my skates without falling on my tail!

Creepella *gracefully* skated onto the ice with the others.

FIGURE SKATING

Figure skating is a sport that involves ice skaters performing jumps, dance moves, and spins on the ice. The Mouslympics has three categories of figure skating: singles, pairs, and ice dancing, which is based on ballroom dancing.

Basic Figure Skating Moves

Competitive figure skating moves include jumps and spins. There are two main types of jumps: toe jumps and edge jumps. Jumps are graded on the position of the skater's feet, the height of the jump, the speed, the landing, and other factors. There are three main types of spins: upright spins, sitting spins, and camel spins, which are performed with one leg extended backward. A skater can earn more points with jumps than with spins.

History of Figure Skating

Ice skating became popular in the thirteenth century in Holland as a way to get around. Skaters traveled from village to village on frozen canals. Around six hundred years later, in 1850, Edward Bushnell invented steel skates, which allowed skaters to make complicated moves and turns. Ten years later, a ballet dancer named Jackson Haines added dance moves to ice skating, and figure skating was born!

Lobelia and Shane's Favorite Moves

Ina Bauer

German ice skater Ina Bauer invented this position, in which a skater's legs are apart and his or her feet point in opposite directions.

Kilian

The Kilian is an Australian couples dance consisting of fourteen steps that are performed very quickly. Both partners perform the steps side by side, in unison.

Couples Camel Spin

Both skaters extend one leg behind them, keeping it parallel to the ice.

Biellmann Position

To perform a Biellmann, the skater moves forward on one foot and grabs the blade of the free skate and pulls it back over his or her head. The skate blade can be held by one or both paws.

I tried to follow her—and immediately fell! This time, my paws got tangled up in my laces.

"Help! My paws are tangled up like spaghetti!" I cried.

Hercule came to my rescue. "Geronimo, get yourself together!" he said.

Anastasia and Paolo skated over to me.

"Look at this mozzarella!" Paolo sneered.

"He doesn't even know how to FASTEN his skates!" Anastasia added.

"They're right! I am bad at sports! All sports!" I wailed.

Lobelia was **ANGRY**. "No, Geronimo, they aren't right. That is bad sportsmouseship!"

She skated over to them

Argh!

like a flash and scolded them. "Athletes need to support one another. We were all **mozzarellas** once! You both started out as beginners, too!"

DANCING ON ICE

I remember when I was a little mouselet. My grandmother Aurelia always told me and my sisters, Topelia and Amelia, about her love of dancing. She would dance with my sisters and me in our garden, and we learned to love dancing, too. Topelia became a classical ballerina. Amelia became a master of gymnastics dance, and I

became a figure skater! And do you know why? One winter day, my grandmother took me to the skating rink in the park. When I saw the snowflakes falling like cotton candy from the sky, and I saw the ice of the lake sparkling like a crystal, I longed to dance on the ice! My grandmother gave me my first pair of skates, and thanks to her, my dream came true.

**LOBELIA TUTU
ICE SKATER**

**TOPELIA TUTU
CLASSICAL
BALLERINA**

**AMELIA TUTU
GYMNAST**

FROM MOZZARELLA . . . TO CHAMPION!

When I was first learning how to ice skate I was a real mozzarella! I fell so often that the other little mice made fun of me and sang "Lobelia Falls Down" to me. Only my friends Thea and Creepella defended me!

I almost quit skating, but my teacher took me aside.

"Lobelia, I know that you have a bright future ahead of you," she said. "Because every time you fall, you always get back up! That is what a real champion does — I swear it on my tail!"

So I didn't give up, and neither did my sisters. We worked hard for many years to achieve our dreams. But we are happy, because we are doing what we love! So if you have a dream, work hard and you will achieve it. Even if you don't become a champion, you will still be a winner — because you'll be doing what you love to do.

I Swear on
My Tail!

After Lobelia **scolded** Anastasia and Paolo, she and Shane took me aside.

"We have a plan," she said. "You and Creepella aren't in this competition to win. You're here to protect the *Silver Skates*! So you don't need to learn any fancy tricks."

"Creepella already knows how to skate," Shane added. "We will teach her some *competition* moves. All you need to do is stay on your feet the whole time."

"**SQUEAK!**" I exclaimed. "That's not **possible**! As soon as I put a skate on the ice, I slip! I don't have any balance!"

"Don't worry, you can learn how to

balance," Lobelia said confidently. "We'll teach you some **balancing** exercises and we won't leave your side until you can stay on your feet by yourself. You'll be able to do it before we finish tonight. I swear on my tail!"

Then she pulled out an enormouse megaphone.

"Forward, Mozzarella!" she yelled. "Let's get moving! I will make you a real skater, I swear on my tail!"

Let's get moving!

Gasp!

"Great job!" Lobelia exclaimed when I had finished. "Now we're ready for the next step: to see if you can balance on the ice. Let's go. The **COMPETITION** is tomorrow!"

I put on my *skates* again and went back onto the rink. Lobelia YELLED instructions through the megaphone.

Heeeelp!

1.
GERONIMO,
STRAIGHTEN OUT
YOUR BACK!

2.
GERONIMO, DON'T
STICK OUT YOUR TAIL!

Is this okay?

Done!

I managed to stay on my feet by gripping the side **rail**.

"**GREAT JOB**, Geronimo!" Lobelia yelled.

She continued to yell instructions:

Argh!

3.
GERONIMO,
DON'T BEND
YOUR KNEES!

Ooooops!

4.
GERONIMO,
DON'T DO
A SPLIT!

I spent the whole day training on the ice. I trained so hard that even my **whiskers** ached! But Lobelia never let me give up.

At one point I **WAILED**, "I can't do it anymore!" and Lobelia skated right over to me.

"Are you a **mozzarella** or a mouse?" she asked. "I will make a real skater out of you, Geronimo! I swear on my tail!"

So I kept training. And by eight o'clock that night, I was able to stand on the ice without **falling** on my tail for more than ten whole minutes!

Creepella **smiled** at me. "Now all you have to do is follow me, Gerrykins," she said. "You'll see that *together* we can do this!"

My friends **cheered** me on.

"Look, he's doing it!" Thea yelled.

"**Great job, Geronimo!**" Hercule said.

"Thank you, friends!" I said happily. "I couldn't have done it without you!"

Lobelia clapped her paws. "That's enough practice, Creepella and Geronimo," she said. "I want you both to have a light and nutritious dinner, and then a **DEEP** sleep. We all need to be rested for tomorrow's competition!"

I called Dr. Fuzz, the health columnist for *The Rodent's Gazette*, to give me some advice about what I should eat that night . . .

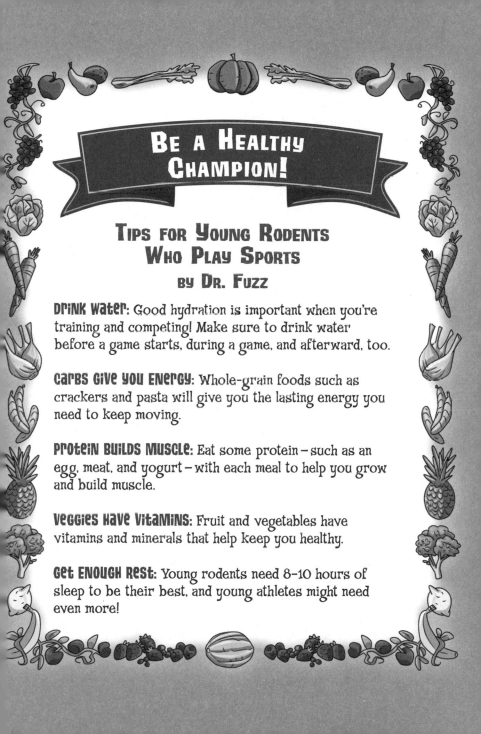

BE A HEALTHY CHAMPION!

TIPS FOR YOUNG RODENTS WHO PLAY SPORTS
BY DR. FUZZ

DRINK WATER: Good hydration is important when you're training and competing! Make sure to drink water before a game starts, during a game, and afterward, too.

CARBS GIVE YOU ENERGY: Whole-grain foods such as crackers and pasta will give you the lasting energy you need to keep moving.

PROTEIN BUILDS MUSCLE: Eat some protein – such as an egg, meat, and yogurt – with each meal to help you grow and build muscle.

VEGGIES HAVE VITAMINS: Fruit and vegetables have vitamins and minerals that help keep you healthy.

GET ENOUGH REST: Young rodents need 8-10 hours of sleep to be their best, and young athletes might need even more!

MAY THE BEST MOUSE WIN!

The next night, it was time for the *championships* to begin! Excited fans filled the stands in the ice arena. And I was **HAPPY** to see that one of the announcers was my friend Dribbler Zestymouse, a soccer expert and a sports writer at **The Rodent's Gazette**!

From the doorway of the locker room, I scanned the arena. I spotted the reason why I was there: the *Silver Skates*. They were displayed in a **SHATTERPROOF** crystal case, where a crowd of rodents ADMIRED them.

Creepella looked around the locker room.

"Remember, one of these skaters might be the thief," she whispered. "We need to keep an eye on them."

Then Dribbler's voice blared through the arena. "Please welcome our first athletes in the pair skating competition, Lobelia Tutu and Shane Shivers! They will be skating to the number 'TANGO FOR TWO.'"

An upbeat tango tune began to play from the speakers. Shane and Lobelia skated around the rink holding paws. Tiny mirrors sparkled on their costumes.

Lobelia and Shane skated *faster* and *faster*, performing a series of skilled moves. It was obvious that they had skated together for a long time.

I looked over at the Silver Skates, and that's when I spotted **Madame No**. When this mysterious mouse shows up, it usually

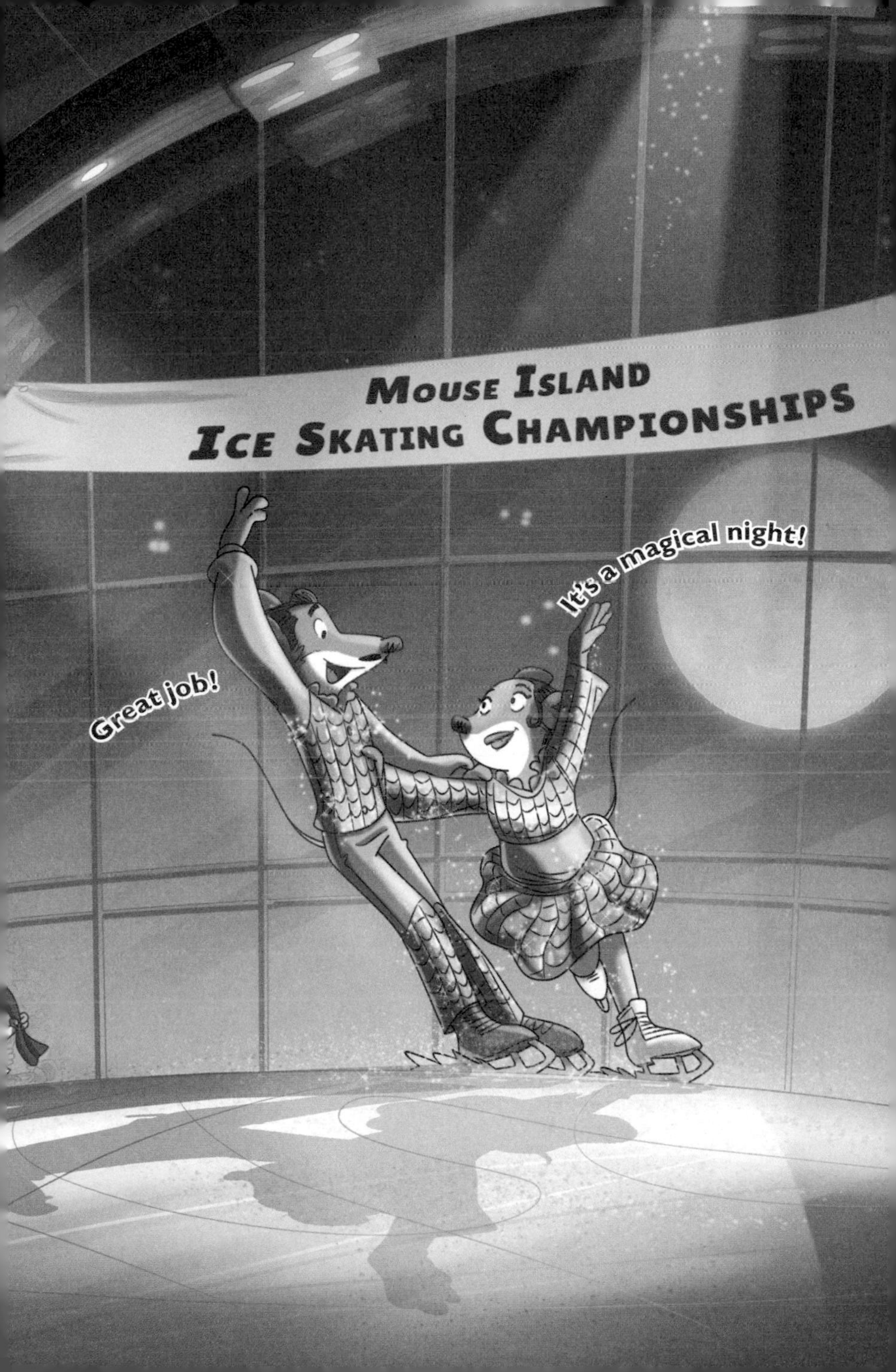
MOUSE ISLAND
ICE SKATING CHAMPIONSHIPS
It's a magical night!
Great job!

means **TROUBLE**! I noticed that she was escorted by two bodyguards, instead of her usual three.

"Creepella, **Madame No** is here," I whispered.

"She could be after the skates," Creepella guessed. "But what's her **plan**? I wonder."

By then, Lobelia and Shane had skated off the ice. The crowd ᴀᴘᴘʟᴀᴜᴅᴇᴅ. Everyone watched as the judges raised their

Wow! The Silver Skates!

signs with their scores. They were all very high!

"Hooray, Lobelia and Shane!" Creepella and I cheered.

"A magnificent performance!" Dribbler cried. He turned to the other announcer. "What do you think, Gary?"

"This team has great technique, Dribbler," Gary replied. "And they got great scores. Is there another team competing tonight who can beat them?"

"We will find out soon, Gary," Dribbler replied. "Up next, here are Felicia Frost and Axel Spinner, who will skate to a song called *Lullaby on Ice*!"

The two glided onto the ice wearing soft white-and-blue COSTUMES that looked like pajamas. Soft, slow music began to play.

Felicia and Axel began to perform a veeeeery slow routine to the veeeeery soothing music.

When the routine ended, Dribbler yawned. "That number was unusual, but very RELAXING. Let's see what the judges say." He gasped. "Oh no! The judges have relaxed too much! They have fallen asleep!"

Bella Twirlytail and Johnny Twizzle entered next, accompanied by some cheerful ROCK-AND-ROLL music. They were

dressed like rodents from the 1950s.

"They will be skating to a tune called 'Rocking Rodents,'" Dribbler announced.

The two began to perform a routine with lots of jumps and spins. The whole stadium kept the beat by clapping their paws and dancing!

"Look at that technique," Dribbler said. "Bella is performing a triple loop jump and . . . it's perfect! Now Johnny is trying the same jump."

Johnny jumped. He spun around three times in the air . . . and he slipped on the landing!

"That mistake will cost them points,"

Gary remarked.

He was right. The judges gave the pair **low scores** for their routine.

Creepella nudged me. "I haven't seen anything suspicious yet," she whispered. "It would take a very bold rodent to steal the skates in plain sight!"

THE DANCING MOZZARELLA

"The next competitors are the mysterious **Masked Skaters**!" Dribbler announced.

"It's our turn, Gerrykins!" Creepella said.

My whiskers began to **tremble**. "Creepella,

Trust me!

I can't do this!" I squeaked. "I can stand on my skates, but that's about all I can do!"

"Trust me, Gerrykins, we've got this," she said sweetly.

She took me by the paw and began to *gracefully* skate around the rink, pulling me with her.

"Just relax, Gerrykins," she instructed.

As she dragged me around, I felt as useless as a rag doll. Luckily for me, she was a great skater!

As we skated, cameras **FLASHED** and the crowd cheered. I broke out into a cold sweat!

"Now the mysterious Masked Skaters will skate to the song, 'THE DANCING MOZZARELLA.' Oh, wait, I mean, 'Bats in Flight.'"

Creepella had chosen a **SONG** written

by the famouse composer Darkwing von Batoven, and performed by the **Spooky Symphony** of Mysterious Valley. It was truly a **HaUNtiNG** tune!

She pushed me into the center of the rink and began to twirl around me.

Just as we had practiced, I began to **wave** my arms in time with the music, just like a **BAT**.

You can do it!

"Interesting performance!" Dribbler said. "The masked gentlemouse is not moving his feet, but is waving his arms in time with the music, while the masked ladymouse skates around him. What do you think, Gary?"

"It's a very beautiful routine," Gary replied. "But they won't score many points unless both skaters perform jumps and spins. At this rate, they will lose the competition."

Luckily, I knew we didn't need to win. All we had to do was protect the Silver Skates.

I kept focusing on my feet, but then a moth landed on my nose. I raised my snout to try to squash it, and that is when I noticed something very, veeeeery, veeeeery suspicious . . .

. . . I saw the shadow of a huge **HELICOPTER** hovering over the glass roof of the arena! "**SQUEAK!**" I yelled. "Why is a helicopter up there?" Then it hit me.

Maybe they were trying to steal the Silver Skates!

I looked for Creepella, but she was skating on the other end of the rink. I waved my arms to attract her attention but everyone thought I was still dancing! I didn't have a choice: I had to cross the rink to warn Creepella about the strange helicopter. There was only problem.

I still didn't know how to skate!

I only knew how to stand up! I shot a look at the Silver Skates, which I had promised to **PROTECT**, and then at the helicopter.

I had to try to skate! So I took one step . . . and I immediately *sliiiiiiiipped*!

Heeeelp!

I slipped with so much force that I did a somersault in midair. But thanks to my balance training, I didn't land on my stomach. **I landed on my paws!**

The crowd burst into applause.

"That was an **IMPECCABLE JUMP**!" Dribbler announced. "The Masked Skater will earn a lot of points for that move!"

"Heeeey!" I yelled, trying to get Creepella's attention, and began to skate. Once again . . .

This time, I somersaulted backward, but I didn't land on my tail. **I landed perfectly**

on my paws!

"Another impeccable jump!" Dribbler said.

Creepella saw me and began to skate at me. I pointed up at the ceiling and tried again to skate to her . . .

I sliiiiiiiipped

This time I launched into the air with a triple somersault.

"Look at this, Gary!" Dribbler yelled. "I've never seen a move like this!"

"A triple jump with a **somersault** and tailspin!" Gary said. "I have never seen anything like that in skating!"

I was sure I was going to land on my tail this time. But Creepella reached me and caught me in the air!

"**Goaaaaaaaal!**" yelled Dribbler, the soccer fan. "I mean, great job!"

The judges raised their **signs**. We had earned a very high score!

"Creepella, there's a **HELICOPTER** above us!" I yelled.

But the crowd was **cheering** so loud that she didn't hear me.

"Go, **MASKED SKATERS**!" they yelled.

Heeeeeeeeelp!

Great job! Super! Fantastic! Cheese-a-rific!

CHAMPIONSHIP JUDGES

Creepella bowed and then turned to me. "Gerrykins, we are a mouserific pair!"

I was about to respond to her that, ahem, we weren't an official couple, and that I was very *worried* about that strange helicopter above us, but she was already pulling me off the ice.

FLYING AWAY IS AGAINST THE RULES!

The crowd quieted down as Anastasia Goudanov and Paolo Pivot *skated* onto the rink!

"Look up! There it is. The **SUSPICIOUS** helicopter I mentioned!" I told Creepella.

She finally heard me and gazed up at the roof. "What is a **HELICOPTER** doing

above the ice rink?" she whispered.

"Do you think it could be part of the **plot** to steal the skates?" I asked.

"Could be," Creepella said. "Let's keep an eye on it and be ready for action."

Anastasia and Paolo skated around the rink, wearing *leopard print* costumes.

"These athletes will perform to '*Waltz of the Gouda*,'" Dribbler announced. "They are dedicating it to Olga Goudanov, an ancestor of Anastasia's."

The two began to skate to the waltz music,

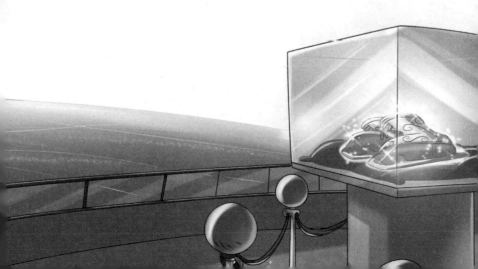

until we heard a . . . **CRAAAAASH**!

Above us, a part of the glass roof shattered into **smithereens**! We heard a metallic groan as a huge **chain** dropped through the hole in the roof. Attached to the chain was a steel cage, and dangling from that was an enormouse hook!

The hook dropped until it hovered above the **SHATTERPROOF** case that protected the *Silver Skates*! At that

Up you go!

moment, Paolo lifted Anastasia above his
head. She jumped off his paws, soared
through the air, and landed on top of the
case holding the Silver Skates!

"OOOOH!" the crowd gushed.

"I'm **very confused**,
Dribbler," Gary said.

"Me, too, Gary,"

Dribbler admitted. "I'm not sure if that move is allowed in the rules."

"Creepella, they are the **thieves**!" I yelled. "We've got to stop them from stealing the skates!"

We both skated toward Anastasia.

Anastasia attached the hook to the case containing the *Silver Skates*.

Dribbler stood up. "Hey, this is **DEFINITELY** not allowed in the rules!"

Meanwhile, we skated toward the glass case at top speed!

Anastasia looked up at

the helicopter. "The skates are hooked—pull us up!" she yelled.

Then she and Paolo quickly **climbed** into the cage.

"*GERRYKINS, JUMP!*" Creepella yelled.

We LAUNCHED off the ice and grabbed on to the cage. Then we climbed in just as the **HELICOPTER** began to lift it into the air.

The chain lifted us through the SHATTERED roof and up toward the helicopter.

The belly of the mysterious helicopter opened and the chain pulled the cage inside. Creepella and I took off our masks. The walls and floors inside the helicopter were covered in *leopard print*. At the controls, a rodent wearing *leopard print* turned around and grinned at us.

"If it isn't *Geronimo Stilton*," she said.

"Hold on to your whiskers, Geronimo. It is I, **Madame No**!"

"I know," I said. "I saw you at the ice arena."

It is I, Madame No!

"Well, maybe *this* will **SURPRISE** you," Anastasia said. She took off her red wig, and I recognized her as **Shadow**, the super spy! Paolo took off his wig and put on a pair of black glasses and I recognized him, too. He was one of **Madame No's** bodyguards!

Shadow laughed. "This **mozzarella** tried to stop us, but he couldn't. We took the *skates* and now the clues to finding the **TREASURE** will be ours!"

"**Mine**, you mean!" Madame No corrected her.

Madame No got up and used a laser tool to

Hmmm...

open up the case holding the Silver Skates.

"Those don't belong to you!" Creepella yelled.

"They do now," Madame No said with a sneer. "**Madame No always wins!** Now what's the secret to the ꭆoyal tꭆeasuꭆe?"

She used a **MAGNIFYING GLASS** with a leopard print handle to examine the **BLADE** of the skates.

There's no map!

"There is no treasure map here!" she snorted angrily. "Just a silly skating scene!"

Then she tossed

the *Silver Skates* over her shoulder!

I quickly sprang into action and caught the skates. Creepella, meanwhile, had taken over the controls of the helicopter. The chain began to drop back down into the arena, and Creepella and I jumped into the cage. We dropped **lower** and **lower** and **lower** . . .

"STOP THEM!" Madame No yelled.

But it was too late. The cage had already touched down onto the **ICE RINK**. Creepella and I climbed out.

I Am Afraid of Heights!

I looked up at the helicopter, which was flying away, and shook my paw at it.

"This doesn't end here! We will see you again — and soon!" I yelled.

Then a crowd of rodents surrounded us, cheering!

Dribbler's voice **BOOMED** over the speaker. "This is incredible! The faces of the Masked Skaters have been revealed: they are Geronimo Stilton and Creepella von Cacklefur."

"And they've saved the *Silver Skates*!" Gary added.

"Squeak," I muttered weakly. "We're

finally on the ground!"

AND THEN I FAINTED!

"Mr. Stilton, wake up!" one of the judges said. They fanned me with their score cards. **"It's time for the awards ceremony!"**

"And now, here are the winners!" Dribbler announced. "In **third** place . . . Bella Twirlytail and Johnny Twizzle! In **second** place . . . Lobelia Tutu and Shane Shivers! And in **FIRST** place, for their incredible acrobatics and for having saved the Silver

Poor mouse!

He fainted!

Argh!

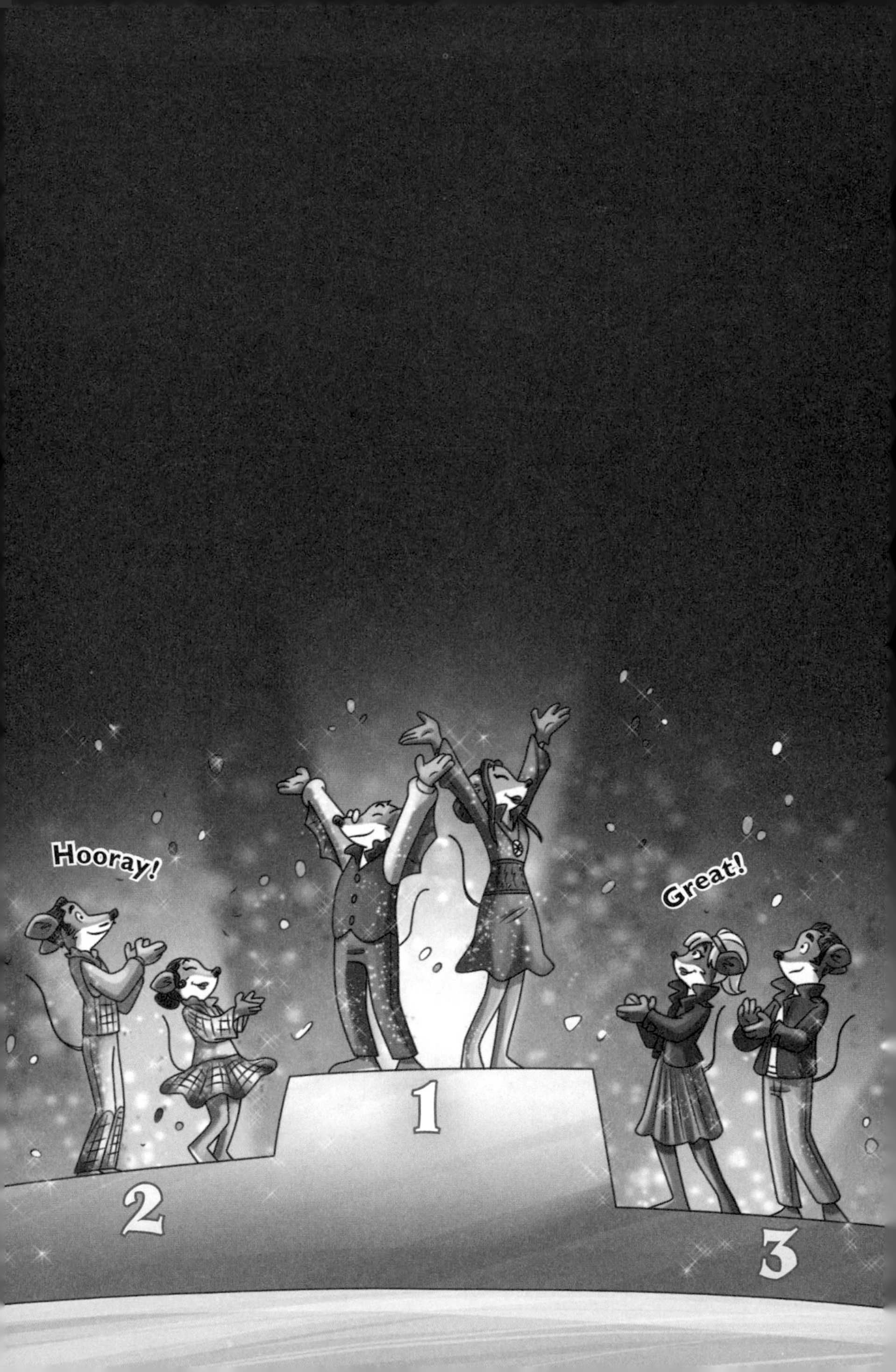
Hooray!
Great!

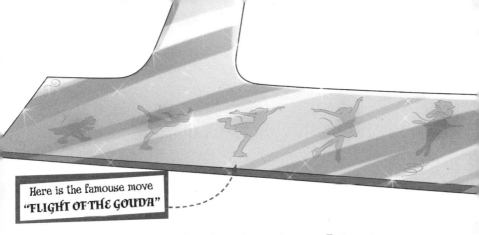

Here is the famouse move
"FLIGHT OF THE GOUDA"

Skates . . . the **MASKED SKATERS**!"

We stepped onto the podium and the judges gave us the prize: THE SILVER SKATES.

After the awards ceremony, Creepella and I EXAMINED the skates with a magnifying glass.

"Gerrykins, look at these carvings on the blade," Creepella said, excited. "This is not a silly skating scene. They show the skating steps that explain how to do Olga Goudanov's famouse move, 'Flight of the Gouda.' This was her treasure!"

The nearby reporters eagerly swarmed us.

"Did you say treasure, Creepella?" one of them asked.

"Yes, but it's not the kind of treasure you think," she replied.

Creepella and I **LOOKED** at each other. We were both thinking the same thing.

"Lobelia Tutu and Shane Shivers should have the skates so they can learn the '𝓕𝓵𝓲𝓰𝓱𝓽 𝓸𝓯 𝓽𝓱𝓮 𝓖𝓸𝓾𝓭𝓪'!" I said.

Lobelia hugged me. "Thank you both," she said. "Shane and I will **STUDY** this move,

and once we understand its SECRETS, we will teach it to our students! We'll do it, I *swear on my tail*!"

"You are so sweet, Gerrykins," Creepella said, and she gave me a peck on the CHEEK, in front of everyone!

The reporters went wild.

"Are you two a COUPLE off the ice?"

"Is the rumor true that you're getting married?"

"We're just very good f-f-friends," I stuttered nervously.

Creepella's eyes twinkled. "That is between us," she told the reporters. "But if we do decide to get married, you will be the *first* to know!"

THE TRUE SPIRIT
OF CHRISTMAS

One week later, **CHRISTMAS EVE** arrived. When I finished decorating the tree, I put two packages underneath, one for Trappy and one for Benjamin. Dear rodent friends, do you know what **gifts** I chose for them? **AH, YOU WILL FIND OUT SOON!** For now, I will tell you that I prepared a **SURPRISE** for them, and I couldn't wait until they opened their presents!

For me the spirit of Christmas is about giving. You don't have to give a present; just telling a special person **"I love you!"** can be the nicest gift of all.

On Christmas morning, I woke up very

early to cook a **Christmas feast** for my friends and family. I made macaroni and cheese, cheese rolls, cheese and crackers, cheese soufflé, cheesy potatoes, and a cheesecake for dessert!

At noon the doorbell rang, and soon my house was filled with **HAPPY** rodents celebrating Christmas!

Finally, the moment arrived to give Benjamin and Trappy their gifts: a pair of

Thank you, Uncle G!

What a great gift!

ice skates for each of them!

They both hugged me. "Thank you, Uncle G! **What a great gift!**" Benjamin said.

"Now open the **GIFT** we all chose for you," Trappy said eagerly.

I opened it and smiled. They had given me a pair of **YELLOW SKATES** the color of **CHEESE**, with my name stitched on them.

I read the tag attached to them: *To Geronimo, who is no longer a mozzarella and has become a real champion! With affection, from all your friends.*

AWESOME!

After our feast, we all went to the park to **ice skate**. This time, I was **EAGER** to get on the ice!

I spent Christmas Day surrounded by my family and friends. As I skated around the pond, I realized that the best gift I had received that year was the gift of friendship. Friendship is the most precious treasure, more precious than even the Silver Skates: because with my friends near me, anything is possible!

I swear on my tail!

The Word of Stilton,
Geronimo Stilton!

Be sure to read all my fabumouse adventures!

#1 Lost Treasure of the Emerald Eye

#2 The Curse of the Cheese Pyramid

#3 Cat and Mouse in a Haunted House

#4 I'm Too Fond of My Fur!

#5 Four Mice Deep in the Jungle

#6 Paws Off, Cheddarface!

#7 Red Pizzas for a Blue Count

#8 Attack of the Bandit Cats

#9 A Fabumouse Vacation for Geronimo

#10 All Because of a Cup of Coffee

#11 It's Halloween, You 'Fraidy Mouse!

#12 Merry Christmas, Geronimo!

#13 The Phantom of the Subway

#14 The Temple of the Ruby of Fire

#15 The Mona Mousa Code

#16 A Cheese-Colored Camper

#17 Watch Your Whiskers, Stilton!

#18 Shipwreck on the Pirate Islands

#19 My Name Is Stilton, Geronimo Stilton

#20 Surf's Up, Geronimo!

#21 The Wild, Wild West

#22 The Secret of Cacklefur Castle

A Christmas Tale

 **#23 Valentine's Day Disaster**

 **#24 Field Trip to Niagara Falls**

 **#25 The Search for Sunken Treasure**

 **#26 The Mummy with No Name**

 **#27 The Christmas Toy Factory**

 **#28 Wedding Crasher**

 **#29 Down and Out Down Under**

 **#30 The Mouse Island Marathon**

 **#31 The Mysterious Cheese Thief**

 **Christmas Catastrophe**

 **#32 Valley of the Giant Skeletons**

 **#33 Geronimo and the Gold Medal Mystery**

 **#34 Geronimo Stilton, Secret Agent**

 **#35 A Very Merry Christmas**

 **#36 Geronimo's Valentine**

 **#37 The Race Across America**

 **#38 A Fabumouse School Adventure**

 **#39 Singing Sensation**

 **#40 The Karate Mouse**

 **#41 Mighty Mount Kilimanjaro**

 **#42 The Peculiar Pumpkin Thief**

 **#43 I'm Not a Supermouse!**

 **#44 The Giant Diamond Robbery**

 **#45 Save the White Whale!**

 **#46 The Haunted Castle**

#47 Run for the Hills,
Geronimo!

#48 The Mystery in
Venice

#49 The Way of
the Samurai

#50 This Hotel Is
Haunted!

#51 The Enormouse
Pearl Heist

#52 Mouse in Space!

#53 Rumble in
the Jungle

#54 Get into Gear,
Stilton!

#55 The Golden
Statue Plot

#56 Flight of the
Red Bandit

#57 The Stinky
Cheese Vacation

#58 The Super
Chef Contest

#59 Welcome to
Moldy Manor

#60 The Treasure of
Easter Island

#61 Mouse House
Hunter

#62 Mouse
Overboard!

#63 The Cheese
Experiment

#64 Magical Mission

#65 Bollywood
Burglary

#66 Operation:
Secret Recipe

#67 The Chocolate
Chase

#68 Cyber-Thief
Showdown

#69 Hug a Tree,
Geronimo

#70 The Phantom
Bandit

#71 Geronimo on Ice!

Don't miss any of my adventures in the Kingdom of Fantasy!

THE KINGDOM OF FANTASY

THE QUEST FOR PARADISE:
THE RETURN TO THE KINGDOM OF FANTASY

THE AMAZING VOYAGE:
THE THIRD ADVENTURE IN THE KINGDOM OF FANTASY

THE DRAGON PROPHECY:
THE FOURTH ADVENTURE IN THE KINGDOM OF FANTASY

THE VOLCANO OF FIRE:
THE FIFTH ADVENTURE IN THE KINGDOM OF FANTASY

THE SEARCH FOR TREASURE:
THE SIXTH ADVENTURE IN THE KINGDOM OF FANTASY

THE ENCHANTED CHARMS:
THE SEVENTH ADVENTURE IN THE KINGDOM OF FANTASY

THE PHOENIX OF DESTINY:
AN EPIC KINGDOM OF FANTASY ADVENTURE

THE HOUR OF MAGIC:
THE EIGHTH ADVENTURE IN THE KINGDOM OF FANTASY

THE WIZARD'S WAND:
THE NINTH ADVENTURE IN THE KINGDOM OF FANTASY

THE SHIP OF SECRETS:
THE TENTH ADVENTURE IN THE KINGDOM OF FANTASY

THE DRAGON OF FORTUNE:
AN EPIC KINGDOM OF FANTASY ADVENTURE

THE GUARDIAN OF THE REALM:
THE ELEVENTH ADVENTURE IN THE KINGDOM OF FANTASY

ABOUT THE AUTHOR

 Born in New Mouse City, Mouse Island, **GERONIMO STILTON** is Rattus Emeritus of Mousomorphic Literature and of Neo-Ratonic Comparative Philosophy. For the past twenty years, he has been running *The Rodent's Gazette,* New Mouse City's most widely read daily newspaper.

Stilton was awarded the Ratitzer Prize for his scoops on *The Curse of the Cheese Pyramid* and *The Search for Sunken Treasure.* He has also received the Andersen 2000 Prize for Personality of the Year. One of his bestsellers won the 2002 eBook Award for world's best ratlings' electronic book. His works have been published all over the globe.

In his spare time, Mr. Stilton collects antique cheese rinds and plays golf. But what he most enjoys is telling stories to his nephew Benjamin.

1. Main entrance
2. Printing presses (where the books and newspaper are printed)
3. Accounts department
4. Editorial room (where the editors, illustrators, and designers work)
5. Geronimo Stilton's office
5. Helicopter landing pad

THE RODENT'S GAZETTE

Map of New Mouse City

1. Industrial Zone
2. Cheese Factories
3. Angorat International Airport
4. WRAT Radio and Television Station
5. Cheese Market
6. Fish Market
7. Town Hall
8. Snotnose Castle
9. The Seven Hills of Mouse Island
10. Mouse Central Station
11. Trade Center
12. Movie Theater
13. Gym
14. Catnegie Hall
15. Singing Stone Plaza
16. The Gouda Theater
17. Grand Hotel
18. Mouse General Hospital
19. Botanical Gardens
20. Cheap Junk for Less (Trap's store)
21. Aunt Sweetfur and Benjamin's House
22. Mouseum of Modern Art
23. University and Library
24. The Daily Rat
25. The Rodent's Gazette
26. Trap's House
27. Fashion District
28. The Mouse House Restaurant
29. Environmental Protection Center
30. Harbor Office
31. Mousidon Square Garden
32. Golf Course
33. Swimming Pool
34. Tennis Courts
35. Curlyfur Island Amousement Park
36. Geronimo's House
37. Historic District
38. Public Library
39. Shipyard
40. Thea's House
41. New Mouse Harbor
42. Luna Lighthouse
43. The Statue of Liberty
44. Hercule Poirat's Office
45. Petunia Pretty Paws's House
46. Grandfather William's House

Map of Mouse Island

1. Big Ice Lake
2. Frozen Fur Peak
3. Slipperyslopes Glacier
4. Coldcreeps Peak
5. Ratzikistan
6. Transratania
7. Mount Vamp
8. Roastedrat Volcano
9. Brimstone Lake
10. Poopedcat Pass
11. Stinko Peak
12. Dark Forest
13. Vain Vampires Valley
14. Goose Bumps Gorge
15. The Shadow Line Pass
16. Penny Pincher Castle
17. Nature Reserve Park
18. Las Ratayas Marinas
19. Fossil Forest
20. Lake Lake
21. Lake Lakelake
22. Lake Lakelakelake
23. Cheddar Crag
24. Cannycat Castle
25. Valley of the Giant Sequoia
26. Cheddar Springs
27. Sulfurous Swamp
28. Old Reliable Geyser
29. Vole Vale
30. Ravingrat Ravine
31. Gnat Marshes
32. Munster Highlands
33. Mousehara Desert
34. Oasis of the Sweaty Camel
35. Cabbagehead Hill
36. Rattytrap Jungle
37. Rio Mosquito

Dear mouse friends,
Thanks for reading, and farewell
till the next book.
It'll be another whisker-licking-good
adventure, and that's a promise!

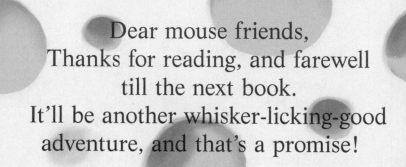

Geronimo